W9-BRJ-694

WOULD I EVER LIE TO YOU?

Caralyn Buehner * pictures by **Jack E. Davis**

Dial Books for Young Readers

My cousin Ed is such a tease;
He says outrageous things with ease.
Mostly they're tales, but *sometimes* they're true!
And so I'm never quite sure what to do.

After supper, just last night,
Ed gave me an awful fright.
In a voice that dripped with dread
This is what my cousin said:

"Please don't eat that piece of pie;
That piece of pie could make you die!
It's full of poison, through and through—
It might just be the end of you!

"If you take a single bite,
First you'll lose your appetite;
You'll feel a burning in your belly,
Your arms and legs will turn to jelly.

"Your tongue will curl, your eyes will pop,
Your hair will fall out with a **PLOP!**
You'll get big lumps and bumps and more
While you're falling to the floor.

"Then you'll die! It's perfectly true.
Would I ever lie to you?"

A poison pie? Could it be true?
With Cousin Ed you never knew.

He once told me he'd watched me hatch
From a big green egg in the cabbage patch.
He said my mother jumped with joy
To find her little alien boy.

Was it true? My mom says not.
But that's the kind of cousin I've got.

One day he stared at me and said,
"There's something strange about your head.
You really ought to do more thinking,
Because it's clear your head is shrinking!"

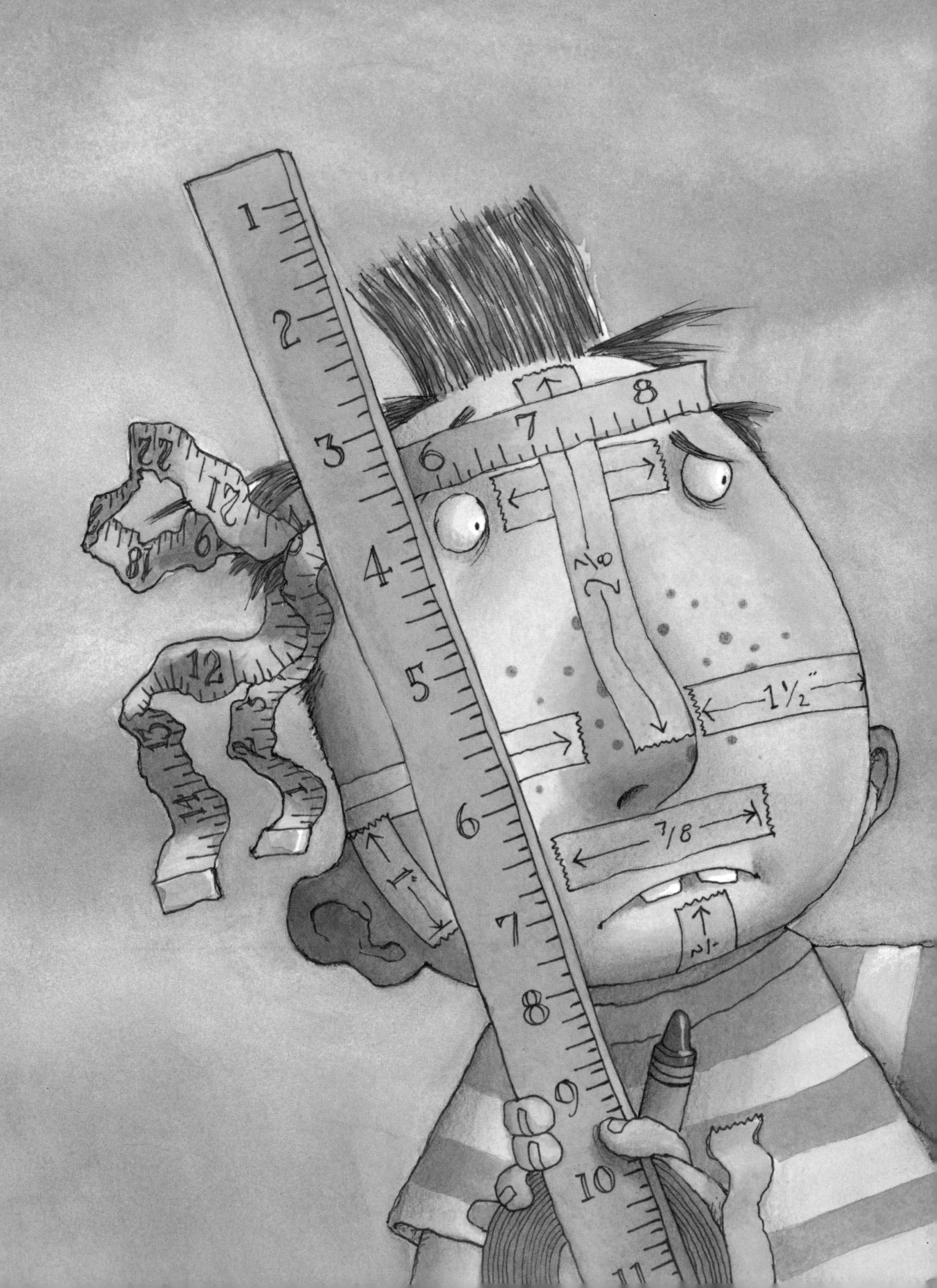

1½"
7/8
1"

I measured my head, I prepared for the worst,
I worried so much that I thought I would burst.
But my head never did shrink smaller in size—
It seems it was just one of Cousin Ed's lies.

Once when we slept at Grandma's house,
Where it's as quiet as a mouse,
I heard loud creaking overhead.
"Don't worry," yawned my cousin Ed.
"It's just the alligators going to bed."

Dad checked everything with a light.
He said, "There's not a thing in sight."
But I still couldn't sleep that night.

When Ed and I were at the zoo,
Ed said, "That monkey looks like you!
When you grow up you'll live here too.
Don't cry, I'll come and visit you."

Was he teasing? I still worry.
I don't want to be all furry!
Ed gave me such an awful fright!
'Cause *sometimes* what he says is right . . .

He said, "Aunt Mary has no teeth."
I thought that was beyond belief.
But when we spied, there was no doubt,
Because we saw her pop them out!

"Your mom has eyes in the back of her head!"
My cookie-snatching cousin said.
I asked my dad if it was true.
"Of course," he said. "All mothers do."

Ed told me there were redwood trees
A car could drive right through with ease.
"No way!" I said, but Mom said yes.
He told the truth that time, I guess.

Ed said, "Hold this big shell a minute.
You can hear the ocean in it."
Well, I knew *that* couldn't be true,
But I listened, and heard it too!

So what about my piece of pie?
Could it really make me die?
Or was it all a silly lie?

Ed said to me, "Here's what I'll do:
I'll eat that poison pie for you."
What a kind, dear cousin true!
Now I knew just what to do.

"Ed," I said, "it's plain to see,
You just want the best for me.
It's time that I took care of *you*.
I'll eat my pie, and then yours too!"

I took a bite, and it was great.
But by that time, it was too late!
I felt a burning in my belly,
My arms and legs all turned to jelly.

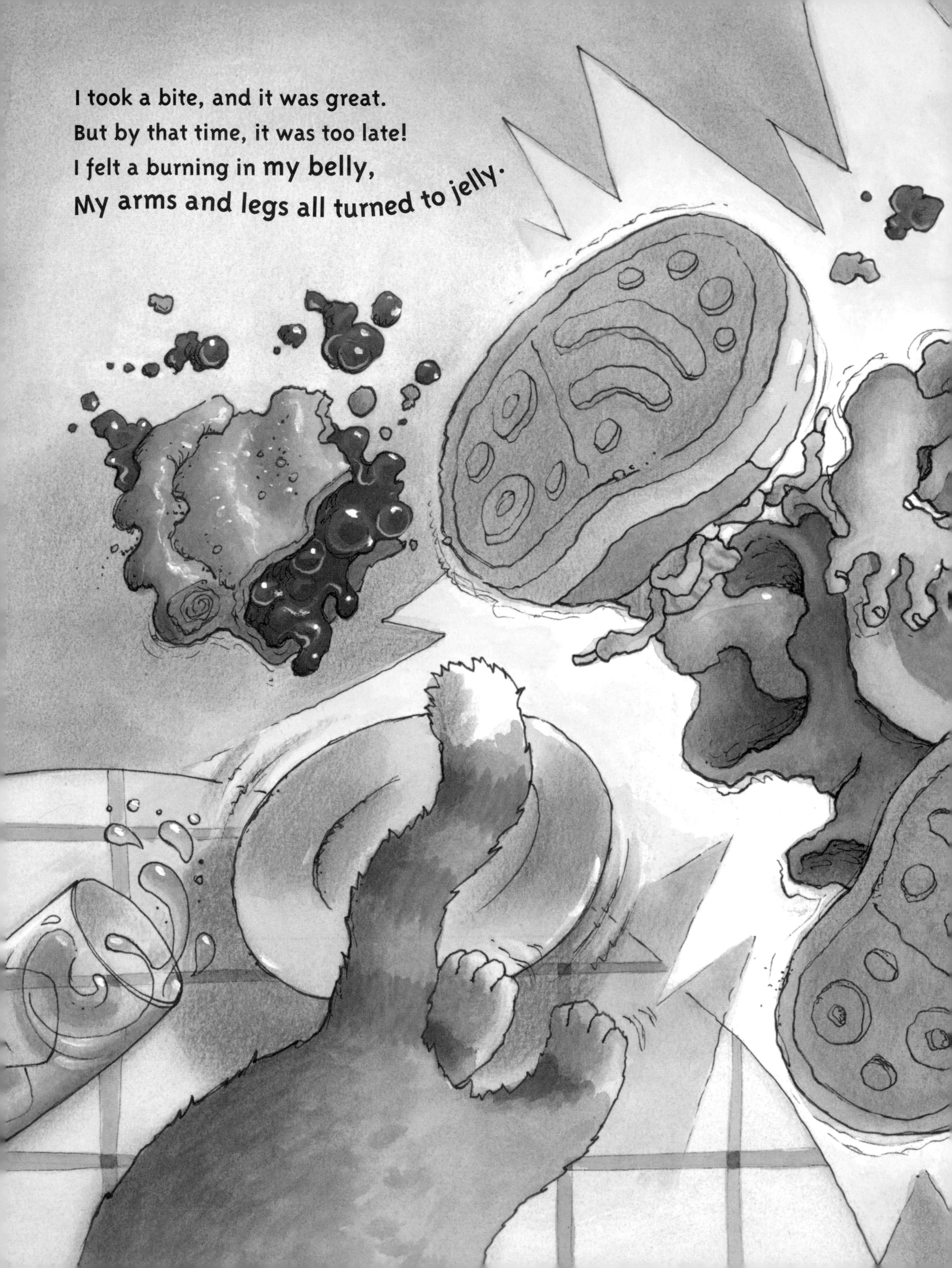

My tongue curled up, my eyes went POP!
My hair all fell out with a plop,
I got big lumps and bumps and more
While I was falling to the floor.

Then I died.
It's perfectly true!

Would I ever lie to you?

For my dad, the tease,
and for Sam, who is following in his footsteps —C.B.

For little Nina.
Would you believe I've dedicated this book to you? —J.E.D.

DIAL BOOKS FOR YOUNG READERS
A division of Penguin Young Readers Group
Published by The Penguin Group
Penguin Group (USA) Inc., 375 Hudson Street, New York, NY 10014, U.S.A.

Penguin Group (Canada), 90 Eglinton Avenue East, Suite 700, Toronto, Ontario, Canada M4P 2Y3
(a division of Pearson Penguin Canada Inc.)
Penguin Books Ltd, 80 Strand, London WC2R 0RL, England
Penguin Ireland, 25 St. Stephen's Green, Dublin 2, Ireland (a division of Penguin Books Ltd)
Penguin Group (Australia), 250 Camberwell Road, Camberwell, Victoria 3124, Australia
(a division of Pearson Australia Group Pty Ltd)
Penguin Books India Pvt Ltd, 11 Community Centre, Panchsheel Park, New Delhi - 110 017, India
Penguin Group (NZ), Cnr Airborne and Rosedale Roads, Albany, Auckland 1310, New Zealand
(a division of Pearson New Zealand Ltd)
Penguin Books (South Africa) (Pty) Ltd, 24 Sturdee Avenue, Rosebank, Johannesburg 2196, South Africa
Penguin Books Ltd, Registered Offices: 80 Strand, London WC2R 0RL, England

Text copyright © 2007 by Caralyn Buehner
Pictures copyright © 2007 by Jack E. Davis
All rights reserved

The publisher does not have any control over and does not assume
any responsibility for author or third-party websites or their content.
Designed by Nancy R. Leo-Kelly
Text set in Triplex
Manufactured in China on acid-free paper
1 3 5 7 9 10 8 6 4 2

Library of Congress Cataloging-in-Publication Data
Buehner, Caralyn.
Would I ever lie to you? / Caralyn Buehner ; pictures by Jack E. Davis.
p. cm.
Summary: A young boy is never sure if his older cousin is teasing or telling the truth.
ISBN 978-0-8037-2793-9
[1. Teasing—Fiction. 2. Cousins—Fiction. 3. Stories in rhyme.] I. Davis, Jack E., ill. II. Title.
PZ8.3.B865Wou 2007 [E]—dc22 2005028223

The art was created using watercolor, acrylic paints, colored pencil, and ink.